Fish Are Not Afraid of Doctors

by J. E. Morris

Penguin Workshop
An Imprint of Penguin Random House

To the staff at MGH and healthcare professionals everywhere—thank you!—JEM

PENGUIN WORKSHOP
Penguin Young Readers Group
An Imprint of Penguin Random House LLC

Copyright © 2018 by Jennifer Morris. All rights reserved. Published by Penguin Workshop, an imprint of Penguin Random House LLC, 345 Hudson Street, New York, New York 10014. PENGUIN and PENGUIN WORKSHOP are trademarks of Penguin Books Ltd, and the W colophon is a trademark of Penguin Random House LLC. Manufactured in China.

Library of Congress Cataloging-in-Publication Data is available.

ISBN 9781524784430   10 9 8 7 6 5 4 3 2

Fish Are Not Afraid of Doctors

by J. E. Morris

Maud went to see Doctor Susan
for a checkup.

Tick Tick Tick

"Do you think fish are afraid of doctors?" asked Maud.

"Fish don't go to the doctor," said Mother.

"I wish I was a fish," said Maud.

"Maud, we're ready for you," said Dr. Susan.

Maud?

"She was here
a second ago,"
said Mother.

Mother heard a small voice coming from the fish tank.

"No one here but us fish," said the voice.

"You know fish don't talk, right?" said Mother.

"Everybody follow me," said Dr. Susan.

"Everything looks good," said Dr. Susan. "All you need now is a vaccination."

"What's a vax-i-nay-shun?" asked Maud.

"It's just a teeny tiny little shot. You will hardly feel it," said Dr. Susan.

"Are fish afraid of vaccinations?" asked Maud.

"I don't think fish need vaccinations," replied Mother.

"I REALLY wish I were a fish," said Maud.

Sigh

Maud shut her eyes.

She pretended
that she had two
floppy fins!

She pretended
that she had
shiny red scales!

She pretended that
she had a swishy,
swooshy tail!

She pretended she
was swimming in
the deep blue sea.

She saw lots of colorful fish.
She even saw a big squiggly octopus.

She found a herd of sea turtles.
She patted their smooth, hard shells.

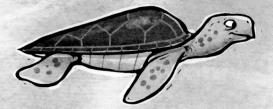

OWWWWWWWWww

She met an enormous whale who
sang her a big whaley song!

AHHHHEEEEEEEEOOOOOOOO

"We're all done," said Dr. Susan.

"We are?" replied Maud.

"See, that wasn't so bad," said Dr. Susan.

"Have a sticker."

"You were very brave," said Mother.

"Don't you know," said Maud . . .

". . . fish are not afraid of doctors!"

Note to Caregivers

No one likes getting shots, but they are sometimes necessary to keep us healthy. Fear of needles is a common childhood anxiety. And as we adults know, the actual pain is usually not nearly as bad as the fear and apprehension leading up to it.

Visualization is an effective strategy for reducing the stress and anxiety. Pretending to be in a soothing place, like swimming through a colorful coral reef, can help relieve tension and calm a child's mind. Encourage children to use all of their senses to help them visualize their happy place. What would they see, hear, smell, and feel if they were really there?

Blowing bubbles is another strategy for dealing with anxiety. Studies have shown that children who have been distracted by blowing bubbles during injections have reported less pain. Blowing on a toy pinwheel, blowing soap bubbles, or just pretending to blow bubbles are all useful distractions.

Your child will most likely never look forward to getting a shot. But by using relaxation and distraction techniques, the process can be made less painful and traumatic for everyone involved.

GRAYSLAKE AREA PUBLIC LIBRARY
100 Library Lane
Grayslake, IL 60030